This book belongs to:

For Delaram and Karim, with admiration, thanks, and love. -*Pippa G*
For Ndut and Kuki. -*Maria C*

Copyright © Tiny Owl Publishing 2022
Text © Pippa Goodhart 2022
Illustrations © Maria Christania 2022

Pippa Goodhart has asserted her right under the Copyright, Designs and Patents Act 1988 to be identified as Author of this work.
Maria Christania has asserted her right under the Copyright, Designs and Patents Act 1988 to be identified as Illustrator of this work.

First published in the UK in 2022
by Tiny Owl Publishing, London

For teacher resources and more information,
visit www.tinyowl.co.uk
#StopTheClockTO

A CIP record for this book is available from the Library of Congress.
ISBN 9781910328828

Printed in China

Stop the Clock!

Pippa Goodhart

Maria Christania

TINY OWL

"Hurry up, Joe. Look at the time!" said Mom. "Where's your other sock?"

"I don't know," said Joe.

"Then find another pair. And put on your shoes."

"Is your book in your bag? Take a piece of toast to eat on the way. Where are my keys? Poppy, let me strap you in. I must put out the trash. What's the time now? Oh, come on, do be quick!"

And, whoosh, slam, Mom, Joe, and Poppy were out of the house, hurrying, worrying, and scurrying along the road.

"Waaaaa!" wailed Polly.

They got to school just in time.
"In you go," said Mom. "Have a lovely day."

"Run, Joe, you're being too slow," said Mom. "We're going to be late."

"Sit down, everyone, quick as you can," said Mr. Khan.

"Look at the time. We haven't got long to get everything done before break time. Put on your aprons. Sit in your places and pick a piece of paper. Now, paint a picture of what you saw on your way to school."

Swish, blue sky, painted Joe. *Up, along, down* gray buildings. *Splurge* red bus, and *whirl* and *whirl* black wheels. *Dot dot* yellow flowers.

Joe was about to paint
Poppy when ...

"Time to stop," said Mr. Khan. "We mustn't be late. Wash your hands. Hang up your aprons. Place your pictures over there.

"Hurry up, Joe. You're being too slow. Look at the clock!"

Tick...tock...tick...tock...

But Joe wanted to include Poppy in his picture.

"STOP THE

CLOCK!

Shouted Joe.

The clock stopped.

Time, and everything else,
stood still ...

... all except for Joe.

Joe took a big slow breath.
He drew Poppy.
Why is she crying?

Then Joe got off
his chair and went
looking at things.

He saw so much more than he'd seen before.
Now he saw that the sky wasn't just bright blue.
There was gray and white and light blue, too.
And there were birds in it.

Plants and tiny creatures made a miniature world.

And the buildings were different, too.
You could tell what sort of people lived
in each one if you looked at the clues.

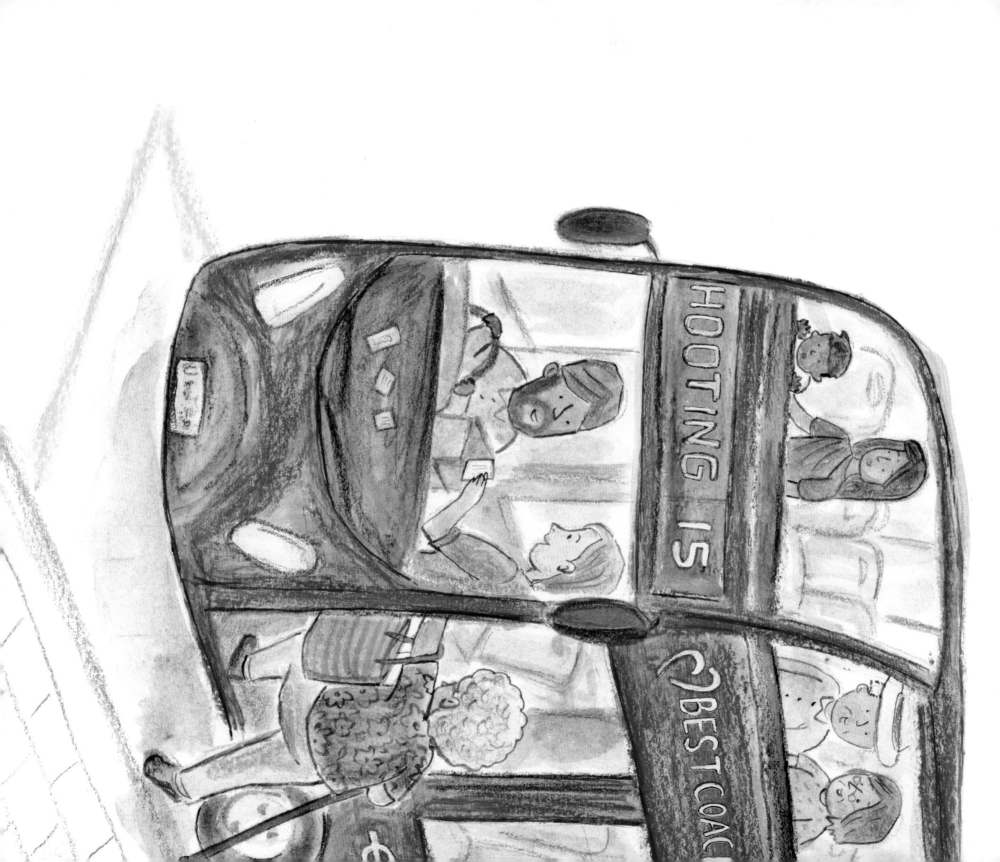

He saw more people, and they were interesting.

He noticed other things. "Poppy's teddy!"

THE CROWN

Joe headed back to school.
He put his picture on the pile.

Tick... tock... tick...

They did.

Then he took a deep
breath and said,
"Clocks, you can
start again now."

Going home, Joe made two people happy.
Their smiles made him happy, too.

"But where are you in your picture?"
asked Mom.

Joe added himself
so that everything
was in his picture.

Everything except for the clock.